DIAROU: NOT SO DIFFERENT

ILLUSTRATED BY ALEX PERKINS

DIAROU BAYO, RILEY CAMPBELL, AND ANTHONY COOKE

Reach Incorporated | Washington, DC

Shout Mouse Press

This book is dedicated to all the strong immigrant children
who feel alone in a new environment. We want you
to know that you are powerful, and you are not alone.

Reach Education, Inc. / Shout Mouse Press
Published by
Shout Mouse Press, Inc.

Shout Mouse Press is a nonprofit writing and publishing program dedicated to amplifying underheard voices. This book was produced through Shout Mouse workshops and in collaboration with Shout Mouse artists and editors.

Shout Mouse invites young people from marginalized backgrounds to tell their own stories in their own voices and, as published authors, to act as leaders and agents of change. In partnership with other mission-aligned nonprofits, we are building a catalog of inclusive books that ensure that all children can see themselves represented on the page. Our 300+ authors have produced original children's books, comics, novels, memoirs, and poetry collections.

Learn more and see our full catalog at www.shoutmousepress.org.

Copyright © 2020 Reach Education, Inc.
ISBN-13: 978-1-950807-11-6 (Shout Mouse Press, Inc.)

FRENCH

Diarou also speaks French. In Guinea, many people learn French in school.

K'ICHE'

Nadir speaks K'iche'. K'iche' is an indiginous Mayan language in Guatemala.

SPANISH

Some of the students in Diarou's ESL class speak Spanish. In the USA, Spanish is the second most common language.

This book is multilingual, just like the characters in it. Learn about the languages in the book.

ENGLISH

A lot of characters in this book speak English. English is the national language of the USA.

MALINKÉ

Diarou's first language is Malinké. Malinké is a language spoken in Guinea, Mali, and a few other West African countries.

We use color-coding for different languages. If you see a word you don't know, that's a great chance to look it up and learn more!

It's my second week in this new school. And my second month in this new country.

Everything is new.

I still can't get used to the dull clothes here. I miss seeing people in colorful pagnes.

I still can't get used to the cafeteria food. I wish they had jollof here.

I still can't get used to taking the Metro to school. I miss walking with my friends.

I wish I could talk to my classmates.

I tried, but I can't understand their English. They speak so fast — like my baby cousin's gibberish!

It makes me feel so...

...alone.

I never felt this way back in Guinea.
I used to have people to talk to.
I used to have my community.

In Guinea, I never felt alone. Habadan.

You could never sit by yourself in the classroom. Somebody would always be talking to you.

Every day at lunch and recess we would play Afro-music. We would dance and compete and laugh.

I miss reenacting soap operas after school with my friends.

I miss performing and learning about different Guinean ethnic groups.

Last night, I told my mom how I felt alone. She told me, "Just because you're from outside a place, doesn't mean you're an outsider." She tucked me in and gave me a kiss. "Alla sinoon nyuman-di i ma."

So today I feel like I have a different mindset. I'm going to my ESL class, where we are ALL in a new place. Are the other kids missing their homes, too? Do they have difficulty speaking this new language? I wonder if there's someone in here who's feeling alone like me.

I walk in and decide to sit with the other kids. They don't notice me. Nobody talks to me. And one kid in the corner just stares at me. His eyes are saying YOU DO NOT BELONG HERE.

I try to talk to the kids. Last week we learned how to introduce ourselves in English: "Hi, my name is Diarou."

"¿Quieres sentarte con nosotros?" Gabriel asks.

I don't know what that means.
My face burns.
I don't know how to respond!
So I do the one thing I told myself I wouldn't do...
I walk away.

I feel so embarrassed.

I take out my headphones and hide in the music.

Every time I'm sad, I listen to K-Pop. The beat takes me away from my problems.

It's time for lunch again. I get in line, which I'm still not used to doing. In Guinea we brought our own lunch or bought from the aunties in the school yard.

Gabriel from my ESL class busts past and gets in front of me. His friends start talking to him, and suddenly a bunch of kids cut me in line! They don't even acknowledge me. Should I do something?

"Fewu! Ce n'est pas juste!"
In my head I am saying: "Excuse me, I was here first. You didn't see me standing here? You need to learn respect!"

I really wish I could say these things out loud! I'm used to sticking up for myself. But now, everything is different.

I feel tears in the bottom of my eyes. I can't even think about food. I run out of the lunch room.

I don't want to go back in there. Maybe I can eat in my classroom. Maybe Ms. LaFuente can help me get something to eat.

On my way to my teacher's room, I'm wondering what the other kids think of me. Do they think I lived in a village? Do they think I didn't have water? Do they think I speak 'African'? They probably don't want to talk to me.

I notice that same kid staring at me. See how he's looking at me? I'm pretty sure he thinks that I'm "champ."

(I learned that word last week when someone made fun of my backpack. At first I thought they were calling me champion. I learned the hard way that I was wrong.)

Why does he have friends and I don't? I feel tears coming out of my heart. I run off to my classroom.

When I get there, my shoulders drop. Ms. LaFuente isn't even here! I thought at least *she* could have been there for me.

"I give up!" I say to the empty room.

I sit on the floor and cry.

Suddenly, I hear someone else crying out
in the hallway. I look out the door and see the
kid who was staring at me.

Why is *he* crying?

Every time I see him he has that mean face,
but now he looks sad like me.

He looks lonely like me.

He looks frustrated like me.

I wish I could help him. I wish I could tell him that he's not alone. But how?

Then I get an idea.

I walk up to him and hand him my headphones.

"Mic Drop!" he says, and his face lights up.
I can't believe he knows this song, too!

He starts dancing like in the video. I unplug the headphones and start dancing, too. I'm surprised that I feel so comfortable around him.

I could get used to this!

About the Authors

Diarou Bayo

My name is Diarou Bayo and I am a fifteen-year-old sophomore at Calvin Coolidge High School in Washington, DC. I really like fashion and I love to do hair. My most important purpose is to make money and make my mom proud. This is my first book. I wrote this story to help kids who have a hard time adapting to a new environment, like I did when I came to this country. I want them to know that just because you are living in a new environment, with people of different backgrounds, it does not make you an outsider. You will always find someone you can relate to.

Riley Campbell

My name is Riley Campbell, and I am 17 years old. I am a senior at Ballou High School in Washington, DC. In my free time I like to do things that involve artistic expression, and I write about topics that may be uncomfortable or not really talked about. This is my second book with Reach and Shout Mouse; I am also co-author of *Man Up!* (2019). I wrote this book because I feel like everyone deserves to be heard, and there's a place for everyone in the world everywhere!

Anthony Cooke

My name is Anthony Cooke Jr., and I'm a junior at H.D. Woodson High School in Washington, DC. I am a bit of a quiet person and I love to be outdoors. This is my first book. I hope that all our readers will enjoy this story that we wrote. We wrote it for you.

Barrett Smith served as Story Coach for this book.
Hayes Davis served as Head Story Coach for this year's series.

About the Illustrator

Alex Perkins

Alex Perkins is a biracial illustrator from small-town Wisconsin who is currently based in Chicago. She received her BFA in Illustration from the Minneapolis College of Art & Design in 2017. Her colorful work explores vibrant fantastical settings, women loving women, and what it means to be human. In her spare time she enjoys learning new things, writing about long journeys, and showering her dog in unearned praise. To see more of her work, you can check out alexpperkins.com.

Writers and artists at work

Acknowledgments

For the eighth summer in a row, teens from Reach Incorporated were issued a challenge: compose original children's books that will both educate and entertain young readers. Specifically, these teens were asked to create inclusive stories that reflect their lived experiences — experiences that this year include the current global pandemic and the struggle for racial justice. As always, these teens have demonstrated that they know their audience, they believe in their mission, and they take pride in the impact they can make on young lives.

Thirteen writers spent the month of July brainstorming ideas, generating potential plots, writing, revising, and providing critiques. Authoring quality books is challenging work at any time, but this year, these young people had to collaborate virtually, during a COVID-19 shutdown. These authors have our immense gratitude and respect: Jocktavious, Daveena, Geralyn, Shatyia, Japan, Damarco, Emilie, Riley, Anthony, Diarou, Danya, Joseph, and Samaria.

These books represent a collaboration between Reach Incorporated and Shout Mouse Press, and we are grateful for the leadership provided by members of both teams. From Reach, Anyssa Dhaouadi, Victoria Feathersone, and Charles Walker contributed meaningfully to discussions and morale, and the Reach summer program leadership of Jusna Perrin kept us organized and connected, even while we all worked apart. From the Shout Mouse Press team, we thank Head Story Coach Hayes Davis, who oversaw this year's workshops, and Story Coaches Barrett Smith, Sarai Johnson, Faith Campbell, and Alexa Patrick for bringing both fun and insight to the project. We can't thank enough illustrators Camryn Simms, Anthony White, Alex Perkins, and Rob Gibsun for bringing these stories to life with their beautiful artwork. Finally, Amber Colleran brought a keen eye and important mentorship to the project as the series Art Director and book designer. We are grateful for the time and talents of these writers and artists!

Finally, we thank those of you who have purchased books and cheered on our authors. It is your support that makes it possible for these teen authors to engage and inspire young readers. We hope you smile as much while you read as these teens did while they wrote.

Mark Hecker,
Reach Incorporated

Kathy Crutcher,
Shout Mouse Press

About Reach Incorporated

Reach Incorporated develops readers and leaders by preparing teens to serve as tutors and role models for younger students, resulting in improved literacy outcomes for both the teen tutors and their elementary school students.

Founded in 2009, Reach recruits high school students to be elementary school reading tutors. After completing a year in our program, teens gain access to additional leadership development opportunities, including The Summer Leadership Academy and The College Mentorship Program. All of this exists within our unique, college and career preparation framework, The Reach Fellowship. Through this comprehensive system of supports, teens are prepared to thrive in high school and beyond.

Through their work as reading tutors, our teens noticed that the books they read with their students did not always reflect their lived experiences. As always, we felt the best way we could address this issue was to put our teens in charge. Through our collaboration with Shout Mouse Press, these teens create engaging stories with diverse characters that invite young readers to explore the world through words. By purchasing our books, you support student-led, community-driven efforts to improve educational outcomes in the District of Columbia.

Learn more at www.reachincorporated.org.

Made in the USA
Middletown, DE
23 November 2020